Bats Past Midnight

A novel by

Sharon Jennings

HIP-JR.

HIP Junior

Library and Archives Canada Cataloguing in Publication

Jennings, Sharon
Bats past midnight / Sharon Jennings.

(HIP jr)
ISBN 1-897039-13-1

I. Title. II. Series.

PS8569.E563B378 2005   jC813'.54   C2005-905374-7

General editor: Paul Kropp
Text design and typesetting: Laura Brady
Illustrations drawn by: Kalle Malloy
Cover design: Robert Corrigan

1 2 3 4 5 6 7   07 06 05 04 03 02

Printed and bound in Canada

High Interest Publishing is an imprint of the
Chestnut Publishing Group

Sam and Simon (the "Bat Gang") have been friends ever since grade two. In their first book, *Bats and Burglars,* the boys caught a couple of crooks who were breaking into a house. In *Bats Out the Window,* they had a chance to be extras in a movie — and that led to extra trouble. Their third book was *Bats in the Garbage.* Sam and Simon were just trying to make some money for a summer fair when they found cash and jewels hidden in a compost bin. Yecch! Now a couple of years have gone by. In *Bats Past Midnight,* Sam and Simon get in trouble one more time!

CHAPTER 1

Midnight Madness

I looked at my best friend, Simon. "I dare you," I said.

"Get lost," he replied. Then Simon pushed his glasses up his nose.

So I glared at Simon and made chicken noises. "*Bwak, bwak, bwak, bwak, bwak!*"

"I'm not a chicken, Sam," Simon told me. "If you want to run around the streets after midnight, go ahead. I'll pass."

"Aw, come on," I said. "It's almost our last night

3

of freedom. Once school starts, we'll be trapped until next summer."

Simon and I were in his backyard, sleeping out. He lives on the street behind mine, a few houses down. The two of us have been hanging out together for years. In the summer, when our parents let us, we sleep outside in the bat house.

The bat house is really just a tree house. We fixed it up when we were little kids and called ourselves the Bat Gang. The Bat Gang is a club with only two members. We have secret codes, a secret handshake and stuff like that. We even caught some crooks and got our pictures in the paper. But that was three years ago.

I looked at Simon. "Bwak?"

Simon threw his pillow at me. "Let's go," he said.

I laughed and peeked outside. No lights were on in any of the houses. We jumped down to the ground and over to the bushes. Then we walked along the fences to the end of our street.

"Where to?" Simon asked.

"Let's go to the park."

We ran down John Street and across Oak. The park was empty this late at night. No little kids and their mommies to bother us.

Simon and I hit the swings. We pumped hard and jumped off, flying through the air. We charged up the slides and ran back down. You can't do that when people are around. You get yelled at by other kids' parents.

I ran over to the sandbox and found a ball someone had left behind. I threw it at Simon's head. A hit! Simon's glasses flew off and he yelled at me. Then he grabbed his glasses, dove for the ball and threw it at my leg. The two of us played catch until we were so tired we flopped down on the grass.

"Hey, Simon! What time is it?"

Simon looked at his new watch. He pressed a button so it lit up.

"It's 2:11:18."

Simon has this cool watch he got for his birthday last week. His watch said it was 11 minutes after 2 a.m. (pretty late) plus 18 seconds. Simon even uses his watch to time stuff. For instance, I know how long he takes in the bathroom. Hey buddy — more than I want to know!

We lay there on the ground, looking at the stars. My breath slowed and I felt really happy. I mean, school was starting and stuff, but being outside at night with your best friend was cool. No one to bother us and everything so quiet. I just felt . . . kind of powerful. It was like the two of us owned the world.

"You want to go back?" asked Simon.

I shook my head. "Not yet. In a minute."

"I'll set the timer."

Simon pushed at the button on his watch. Sure enough, the watch went *beep*. "Time's up. Let's go." Sometimes Simon is a real pain.

Then we heard another sound. Some kind of car was coming down the road, moving slowly. It wasn't like a normal car would go.

"Maybe it's our parents, looking for us," Simon said.

I nodded. Simon and I have gotten into lots of trouble over the years. We've caught burglars and crooks, but our parents were still mad at us. It can be tough being a hero.

"If Mom and Dad catch us out here, we're dead meat," I said. So we snuck off into the bushes and waited.

A car pulled up to the curb. It didn't have any lights on.

"It's not your parents or mine," Simon said. "They'd have the headlights on."

I nodded. "Let's get out of here."

Simon grabbed me and pulled me down. "Are you crazy? What kind of guy rides around in a dark car at . . ." Simon checked his watch, "at 2:22:08?"

I was going to say "who cares" but then we heard another car coming. I could see it pull up beside the first one. The first car was black with blacked-out windows. The second car was a bright yellow Corvette.

We sat and watched as a man got out of the first

car. He went over to the window of the yellow car and leaned in.

"Maybe he's a cop," I whispered. "Maybe it's an undercover thing."

Simon shrugged. When both cars drove away, Simon checked his watch. "2:24:01," he said. "Less than two minutes. That's pretty strange."

We waited for a while to make sure the two cars didn't come back. Then Simon and I started for home. We crossed the street right where the cars had been parked. That's when Simon grabbed my arm.

"Ow!" I yelled.

"Shhhh!" whispered Simon. He bent down and picked up something from the street. At first, we couldn't see what it was. But Simon took it over to a street lamp, and then we knew.

Simon had found a wad of cash.

CHAPTER 2

House Arrest

"Wow!" I whispered. "How much is there?"

Simon counted the bills.

"One thousand dollars," he told me. Then he looked down the street. "Those two guys in the cars must have dropped it."

"But it's ours now, right?" I asked. "We found it, right?"

"I don't know," replied Simon. "We'll have to go to the police."

I grabbed the money from his hand. "We can't

11

go to the police," I whispered. "We can't tell anybody we're out this late."

Just then we heard another car. Without even saying a word, Simon and I jumped behind a tree. The car kept going, so Simon and I crept out of hiding.

"Come on," said Simon. "Let's get out of here."

I shoved the money into my pocket. We hurried home, keeping to the bushes and fences, just in case the yellow car came back.

When we got to Simon's backyard, all of his house lights were on. My parents and Simon's were standing by the bat house.

"Don't tell them about going to the park," I hissed at Simon. "Not a word about the cars or the money, okay?"

Simon nodded, and then we were ready. As soon as we got in the yard, both sets of parents were all over us.

"You two . . ." my mom started. She was so mad that she began to choke up.

My dad joined in. "You two idiots! You two

little . . . " Then my dad stopped and got choked up like my mom.

Simon's parents took over. "We didn't know what to think! How could you! We trusted you!"

"We didn't do anything," I told them all. "We were just, you know, goofing off."

"Goofing off?" said Simon's mom. "Goofing off?!" Our parents kept yelling as they dragged us to our homes.

Back home, I told my parents that Simon and I couldn't sleep. I said we just went out hopping fences. I sure hoped Simon told his parents the same thing. I mean, what if he said we were hungry? What if he said we went to the all-night pizza place?

As soon as I was alone in my room, I took out the money and counted the bills again. Yup. Simon was right. There were ten hundred-dollar bills. I'd never seen a hundred-dollar bill before, much less ten of them. A thousand dollars! I started thinking about what I could do with so much money. Buy a new Nintendo system, for sure.

Man! I really needed to talk to Simon. But the next day, I had to stay in my room. My folks wouldn't even let me call Simon on the phone.

"Think things over," said my dad.

"And clean up your room," said my mother.

Great way to spend the last day of summer vacation!

So I sat there, listening to some music. I shoved some clothes out of the way and threw some stuff into a box. Then I took the wad of cash out from under my bed and counted it again. *Simon, buddy, what are we going to do?!*

Then I had a good idea. First, I shoved the money into my desk. It was pretty messy in there. Paper, gum wrappers, lots of junk. Then I opened my window and hissed at my sister.

"Ellen! Ellen! Come up here. I need you."

Ellen was playing out in the wading pool in our backyard. "What do you want?" she yelled. It was her bratty little sister voice.

"SHHHH! Just come up."

Ellen jumped out of the wading pool and came

inside. She was dripping wet. Great. She'd leave a trail of water all the way up to my room. I opened my door and pulled her inside.

"You have to take a note to Simon."

"You're not allowed to talk to Simon," Ellen whined. "Mom said."

I made a face. "Mom said I couldn't *talk* to Simon. She didn't say I couldn't *write* to him."

Ellen made a face back at me. "Pay me or I'll tell."

So I agreed to pay her a dollar.

I had already written the note. It was in Bat code. Simon and I made up the code four years ago when we started our club. I used to know how to write it fast, but now I needed some help. So I wrote out all the vowels like this:

A   E   I   O   U   Y

Then, under them, I wrote out all the vowels backwards, so it looked like this:

A E I O U Y
Y U O I E A

And then I wrote my note to Simon, changing all the vowels — top to bottom. Simon's name came out *Somin*. My name is Sam so it comes out *Sym*. Get it?

But then Simon and I made the code a little bit harder. We wrote everything backwards. So Simon became *Nimos*. Sam comes out *Mys*. I tell you, we used this code a lot to send notes in school. Even if our teacher caught the note, he could never figure it out.

Nimos.
    Kcets no am miir. In upycsu. In VT. Tyhw teiby aunim?

                       Mys.

Simon. Stuck in my room. No escape. No TV. What about money? Sam.

Pretty soon, Ellen was back.

"Here's a note for you," Ellen said. "I made Simon pay me a dollar, too."

Mys.

Um iit. My gnodyur kiib. Udoh aunim.

Nimos.

Sam. Me too. Am reading book. Hide money, Simon.

A book?! That was just like Simon. He didn't even mind being stuck in his room. It gave him lots of time to read. Why read when you can be out having a good time, I say.

So I sent another note back to Simon.

Nimos.

Doh aunim. Tuum um wirrimit ty 8:30.

Mys.

It cost me another dollar.

Simon's reply said: Ayki. And Ellen made him pay again.

Then my mother knocked on my door. I don't know why she bothered to knock because she just barged right in.

"What's going on with you and Simon? What's with all these strange notes? Are you two up to something?"

Simon. Hid money. Meet me tomorrow at 8:30. Sam.

"How'd you find out?" I asked.

"Ellen told me."

"Ellen? But I paid her!" I said, angry as anything. "Tell Ellen I'm going to kill her!"

"Sam, answer my question."

"You won't let me talk to Simon, so I had to send a note. We're just making plans to walk to school tomorrow."

My mom looked around the room. "When are you going to clean up this place?" she asked.

I looked around my room, too. "I did clean up."

My mom rolled her eyes. "Sam, clean up this room or you'll stay in here until you do." Then she left and slammed the door.

So I cleaned up my room even more. I picked my clothes off the floor. I put some in my closet and threw some in the garbage. I emptied my knapsack. Then I found my lunch from the last day of school. It wasn't looking too good. I went under my bed for candy wrappers and pop bottles. Then I found a book I told my parents I'd lost. They paid the school for it and here it was — *The Mystery of the Missing Money.*

Then I sat down on my bed and stared at the wall. I thought about those guys we saw last night. I knew they'd be really steamed when they found out they'd lost their money. I wondered if they had seen us. And all that made me a little nervous.

CHAPTER 3

First-Day Foul-Up

I woke up early the next day and got dressed right away. It was the first day of school. I put on my oldest pair of jeans. I topped it with my very best T-shirt, the one that said "Eat. Sleep. Play Hockey." I wondered what Simon would be wearing. Last year, he wore a T-shirt that said "I Love School." He better not pull a stunt like that again!

I grabbed my lunch and headed over to Simon's house. I was glad to see his T-shirt read, "Bad to the Bone in Drumheller." Now *that* was cool.

"Hello, Sam," said Mrs. McDonald. "I was just telling Simon to hurry up. I'll drive you boys to school."

What? We're in grade six and Simon's mommy has to take us to school? No way! I glared at Simon and yanked him out the door.

Our school, Hilltop P.S., is built on a hill. The back of the schoolyard runs down a steep slope to the road below. The slope used to be just mud, but a few years ago all us kids planted trees and grass back there.

Simon and I had a secret hangout on the slope.

It was halfway down the hill and around the corner from the main schoolyard. It was a small hollow cut into the hill. It had bushes and weeds in front of it. We called it the Bat Cave.

Simon and I would never go to the Bat Cave together. And we never went straight there. We separated and then zigzagged to get there. This made it harder for anyone to follow us. I saw that once in a war movie.

I zigzagged to the Bat Cave and heard Simon sneezing from halfway down the hill. Simon has hay fever. In the fall, he sneezes a lot.

"What time is it?" I asked him.

Simon checked his watch. "8:31:23 . . . oops, now it's 8:31:26. Funny how time flies."

"So we'll stay put until 8:56:59. Then we can get to class just in time," I told him. We wanted to look cool on the first day. Not too eager to get to class.

"So where's the money?" he asked.

"Relax. I hid it in my drawer. The drawer is crammed with junk. No one will ever find it there."

Simon nodded and sneezed. Then he looked outside the Bat Cave. "Sam! It's the car!"

I looked past the bushes and down the hill. There it was, parked on the road below. I could see the Corvette better in the daylight. It was bright yellow and had really big wheels. The windows were black and there were silver lightning bolts on the doors.

"It's the exact same car we saw the other night," I said.

"What are we going to do?" Simon asked. "Maybe we should go down there and give the guy his money back."

I thought about all that money sitting in my desk.

"Not yet," I said. "We don't know for sure it's his money. And there's something a little weird about this guy."

"Then we should go to the police," said Simon. "We don't have to tell them *when* we found the money."

"Let's just wait a while, okay?"

Simon sighed and said okay. Then he looked at the car again.

"Man," he said. "If my mom had a car like that, I'd let her drop us off at school every day. I'd even yell 'bye, Mom' so all the kids would know it was my car."

So we sat there watching the Corvette. And just as it drove off, we heard the bell ring.

"What time is it?" I yelled.

"Nine o'clock," he said. "I mean, 9:00:08!"

"Yikes!" No time to zigzag. Simon and I ran like crazy for the school.

Our new classroom was on the second floor. We threw ourselves in the door, just as everyone stood for *O Canada*. Mr. Chong rolled his eyes when he saw us. When everyone sat down, Mr. Chong yelled at us for being late. We expected that. But the other kids looked at us as if we were cool. Late on the first day. Way to go! And then it got even better.

Mr. Chong held open the door. "I'm not putting up with this. You two can go to the office."

Now we were *really* cool.

CHAPTER 4

Busted!

The next few days at school were lousy. Something always seemed to backfire on us. At recess on the first day, all the kids were talking about the big summer fair. Bat enemy #1, Jim Brody, had been there. He had seen me get on the merry-go-round with my sister, Ellen.

"Hey, Simon," Jim yelled. "Maybe your T-shirt should read 'Eat. Sleep. Baby-sit!'"

"My dad made me!" I replied. "I had to help my sister!"

All the kids laughed anyway.

The very next day, Jim Brody pantsed me. He pantsed me so hard I fell right over. I yanked my jeans up real fast, but not before I heard lots of giggling. *Oh great,* I thought. *How much did the girls see?*

The next day, Simon and I got picked *last* for baseball. Jim Brody laughed, "You guys suck at baseball," and that was true. But was it fair?

When it rained on Thursday, my mom drove us to school. Did she have to yell "love you" out the window?

Simon and I met for lunch each day in the Bat Cave. We both felt lousy.

"This is just great," I said. "All the kids think we're a couple of dorks."

"They wouldn't if we could get a ride in that Corvette." Simon pointed down the hill. The yellow car was back again. "It shows up each day at the same time," Simon said.

"What are you doing?" I asked. "Timing it?"

"Yeah. Yesterday it showed up at 12:33:25. It

stayed until 12:52:19. See? I wrote it down."

I looked at a dirty piece of paper. The paper looked like Simon had sneezed all over it. "What are these other times for?"

"Each time that car shows up, kids from the high school go over. They talk to the driver, and I time them."

Simon was right. Two older kids leaned into the car window. And then, in a couple of minutes, or at 12:42:49, they walked away. Then at 12:45:02, another teenager came along.

"Big deal," I said. "The high school is just around the corner." And then I had a great idea. A Bat brainwave. "I'm going to check it out. I'm going to go down there and walk right up to that car."

"Are you nuts?" Simon asked. "Remember what we saw the other night? I think the driver is up to something. Don't forget, we've got *his* thousand dollars."

"But if we could get a ride in that car, we wouldn't be dorks. We'd be cool again. So I'll just ask the guy. I'll tell the guy he's got a great car. Then I'll ask him to drive me back to the schoolyard."

"And you think that will work?" Simon asked.

"Sure. I'm just a little kid drooling all over his car. He won't mind showing off."

"Maybe you should give him his money back for a ride in his car," Simon said.

I thought about the money in my desk. Every morning and every night I took out the money and just looked at it. I kept dreaming about what it could buy. No way I wanted to give it back.

"Uh . . . yeah . . . maybe," I said. "Look. If I get a ride in his car, then maybe I'll know what to do about the money. Like, I'll find out if it's his or not."

Simon shook his head. Sometimes, I think he doesn't trust me.

At lunchtime the next day, Simon and I hid out on the hill. At 12:47:09 the yellow car showed up.

"I'm off," I said.

"But lunch is almost over," Simon pointed out.

"Don't worry."

I snuck out of our spot and ran from bush to bush down the hill. When I got to the bottom, I swung myself over the fence and hit the sidewalk. I ran down the street and walked right up to the car.

I tapped on the window.

The driver rolled it down.

"Get lost, kid," he said.

"Um, hi, like I was hoping you could show me your car," I said.

"You're looking at it, kid. Now get lost."

The driver was really big. His head touched the roof and his body filled the whole seat. He wore dark sunglasses.

But just then, I heard the warning bell ring. Only five minutes before we had to be inside. Time was getting short!

"Please, sir. I've been watching you for days and I really like your . . ." But I didn't get to finish. The driver stuck his hand out the window and grabbed my shirt.

"You what? You been watching me?" the guy

yelled at me.

I tried to shake off his hand, but it didn't work. "Well, your car, I mean. I mean your car is so neat and . . ."

I didn't get to finish. Just then a police car came around the corner. In no time, the yellow car took off. I was really glad the guy let go of me before he burned rubber.

I thought the cop car would go after the yellow car, but it didn't. Instead, this great big cop got out of his cruiser and came over to me.

"Hey kid! What are you doing down here?" he asked.

"Um, nothing. I was just . . ." I began.

"Are you skipping school?"

"No sir, I just . . ." But I didn't get to finish. The cop shoved me into the backseat of the cruiser.

"Know what we do with little punks like you?" he asked.

"No sir."

"We throw you in jail!"

CHAPTER 5

Brainstorm

Jail! This was awful! What would I tell my parents?

Then I started thinking. Maybe jail wasn't so bad. I mean, I wouldn't have to put up with Jim Brody making fun of me. Then I thought of something even better.

"Would I miss school?" I asked.

The cop laughed.

"I'm just pulling your leg, kid," he said. "I'll just

give you a ride up to school. That's a pretty big hill there."

Rats!

The cop drove around to the front of the school. Simon was standing with a bunch of kids at the school door. He was blocking the door, waving his arms and pointing to the street.

Good old Simon. He was holding the kids back so they could see me get out of the yellow Corvette. Too bad he didn't know what happened.

The cop got out of his door. Then he came around and opened my door. I stepped out and all the kids stared at me. Simon's mouth fell open.

Jim Brody pointed at me. "What did you do, Sam? Steal a little kid's lunch?"

All the kids laughed.

"Shouldn't you all be in class?" asked the cop.

Simon stopped guarding the door. He opened it and the kids went inside.

The cop turned to me.

"What's your name, kid?"

"Sam, sir."

"Well, Sam. Don't let me catch you skipping class again, okay?"

I nodded and ran inside. I zoomed up two flights of stairs and into my classroom.

Mr. Chong was not thrilled. "In trouble again?" he asked.

Mr. Chong did not wait for an answer. He started with some math but I couldn't keep my mind on it. I kept wondering what I'd tell the kids at recess.

Then the kid behind me poked me with her pencil.

I turned around to glare but she handed me a piece of paper.

Tyhw dunuppyh?

I tore a hunk of paper out of my notebook. This is what I wrote back.

What happened?

Tig it ryc. Pic umyc. Ryc kiit ffi. Pic dubbyrg um.

I was watching Simon read it, so I didn't see Mr. Chong come down the aisle. But I sure heard his ruler when he banged it on my desk. I spun around fast. But Mr. Chong was halfway to Simon.

"Give me that note, Simon" he said.

Simon handed it over and Mr. Chong threw it into the garbage can.

"Sam and Simon — half hour with me after school," he said.

Great. Could this day get any better?

The afternoon dragged on. We finished math and started social studies.

"For this unit we're going to look at careers," said Mr. Chong. "Your project is to learn about the job of someone in our town. You can work with a partner on this. I want a written report and an

Got to car. Cop came. Car took off. Cop grabbed me.

oral presentation. The written report has to be two pages long. The presentation should last about ten minutes. Any questions?"

There were lots of questions. Most of them were stupid.

"When's it due?"

"How long does it have to be?"

"Is the written thing due at the same time as the oral thing?"

"What's it about?"

Mr. Chong rolled his eyes. He went over the project again. Then he told us to find a partner. I picked Simon, of course. I don't think Mr. Chong wanted us to work together, but there was no choice. No one else ever wanted to work with us.

Mr. Chong gave us ten minutes to figure out our topic. But all Simon and I did was talk about what happened to me.

"That guy was huge," I whispered to Simon. "And he grabbed me, like hard."

"Were you scared?" he asked.

"Nah," I lied. "But you were right. There's something creepy about him."

Then Mr. Chong was right beside us. "You boys having a nice chat?" asked Mr. Chong.

And so Simon and I got back to the stupid project. Simon kept coming up with ideas. I kept saying that they were all boring. So at the end of the time, we had nothing.

Mr. Chong asked us all what we had chosen.

Two kids had chosen the school nurse. Someone else picked a bus driver. Jim and Haji were going to talk to the guy at the corner store.

Simon elbowed me. "What are we going to do?"

I shrugged.

Simon hissed in my ear. "My dad's a dentist. Let's do him."

"Are you crazy? Who wants to learn about a dentist?"

"Well what then? We've got thirty seconds!"

The last thing I wanted to think about was some stupid project. I had plenty of other stuff to worry about. I had to figure out some way to explain being in the cop car. I had to do something about that money we found. And then . . . I don't know how it happened, but I got a really good idea. A Bat brainstorm. One that solved everything.

Mr. Chong stood in front of us.

"Well, boys? What's your topic?"

Simon started to talk, but I elbowed him.

"Simon and I are going to do a report about the police," I said. Then I looked at the rest of the class. "That's why I was in the cop car."

CHAPTER 6

Ambush!

Mr. Chong was amazed. "How could you start the project this morning? I just gave it to you."

Simon didn't help. Did he have to sit there with his mouth hanging open? He looked like a dork.

"Well . . ." I thought fast. "I heard about it from some kids last year."

Mr. Chong rolled his eyes and walked away.

Whew! Close call!

At recess, we couldn't go to the Bat Cave. Too

many kids came up and wanted to know if I was telling the truth.

"Of course I'm telling the truth!" I shouted. "I know lots of cops. It goes back to when me and Simon were heroes."

Then all the kids shut up. They knew about us catching crooks a few years ago.

When they left us alone, I turned to Simon. "Am I a genius or what?"

"It's pretty good, Sam. We do know some police officers. And . . . yeah, I think you've come up with a good plan."

For the first time in a long time, Simon and I gave each other the Bat handshake. This is where I link his thumb with my thumb and we wave our fingers. Our hands together form a bat, see?

When school ended, Mr. Chong changed his mind. "You don't have to stay after. You two give me a headache. Go on home."

So Simon and I raced home. It only took us 5:11:13. That's five minutes, 11 and 13/100 seconds, in case you wanted to know. We told our moms we

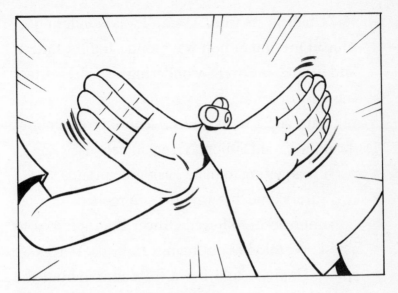

had to go to the police station.

"Why? What did you do now?" my mom asked.

Very funny.

We hopped on our bikes and were at the station in 6:32:18. We knew just where it was because we'd been there lots of times before. It's like I said.

We didn't have to stand around too long before someone came over to us. I guess they don't get kids coming in all the time.

"I'm Officer Brannon," said this one cop. "What can I do for you?"

"Uh, hello, ma'am," I said. "I was wondering . . . I mean me and Simon was wondering . . . I mean Simon and me were wondering . . . " I sort of trailed off.

"Sam and I want to do a school project about the police," said Simon. "Can you help us?"

"I was getting to that," I said to Simon.

"Sure. Come this way," the cop replied.

Simon and I followed Officer Brannon over to a desk. We told her our names and what school we go to. Then we told her a little more about the project. She gave us some stuff to read.

"This is all about your local police force," she said. "It will give you lots of basic ideas. Anything else?"

"Thanks, ma'am," said Simon. Then he stood up. But I had a better idea.

"I was wondering if you could come to our school? You know, sort of like show-and-tell."

Officer Brannon smiled. "I might be able to do that." She nodded her head. "That might be kind of fun."

So we told her we'd talk to Mr. Chong. Then maybe we could set a date.

And that was that! We were back on our bikes and zooming along. Our project was just about done!

"We have to read the stuff she gave us," warned Simon.

"Yeah, yeah."

"I mean it, Sam," Simon told me. "You had a great idea, but we can't blow it. We could get a really good mark, for once."

"I said I'd read it, okay?" Sometimes Simon is a real pain.

I figured I'd get around to it next week, no hurry. But then I found out my parents were going to keep me grounded over the weekend. I said Simon and I had to work on our project. So we got to hang out a bit, even if my mom kept sticking her head into my room to see if we were really working. And we *were* working, mostly. Except for all the time we spent looking at the money.

On Monday we talked to Mr. Chong. He really

liked our idea of bringing in the cops as part of our report. So then we biked back to the police station after school. We talked to Officer Brannon again. And soon the whole thing was set up for Thursday.

The next day, Simon and I headed to the Bat Cave at recess.

"You know, I might become a cop when I grow up," I told Simon.

"I thought you wanted to be a hockey player."

"Well, when my NHL career is over. Then I'll be a cop."

Simon started to say something, but just then the yellow Corvette pulled up. Simon wrote the time down. 12:37:18. After a while, the big guy got out and stretched.

Then, Simon sneezed.

The big guy looked up. He shaded his eyes from the sun. He kept staring up at the hill.

The two of us sat really still. We were hidden behind some bushes.

"I don't like this," Simon whispered.

"Shhh," I whispered back. "He can't see us. Just

don't move. And don't sneeze!"

But of course, Simon did. A real snotty sneeze. A real wet, disgusting one.

"Hey, kid," shouted the guy. "I told you to stop watching me."

Then the bug guy bent down and picked up something off the road. I saw him bring his arm back and fling something at the hill. Stones! The creep was throwing stones at us! One landed real close. Thud! Then another and another. One hit the ground by my foot. Then I heard Simon make a funny sound. I looked at him.

Blood.

Simon had been hit.

CHAPTER 7

Road Apples

I stared at Simon's forehead. It was still bleeding.

I didn't know what to do. I was afraid to move. It seemed like ages before the creep got in his car and drove away. When we were able to sneak out of the Bat Cave, recess was long over.

We ran to the washroom. Simon wiped away the blood. It wasn't a big cut, but I could tell he was scared. So was I.

"Do we tell somebody?" I asked.

Simon shook his head. "We'll get in trouble for

having a secret hangout. And my folks will kill me for spying on that car."

So Simon and I went back to class. Simon said he'd fallen down. He said we were late for class because we were cleaning up the cut. Mr. Chong rolled his eyes. He sure rolls his eyes a lot.

I never wanted to go back to the Bat Cave again, but Simon did. He didn't say much, but I could tell he was really mad. Every day he snuck off by himself and wrote down all the times the car showed up.

"Why are you doing this?" I asked. "Who cares about that jerk?"

"He's up to no good," Simon said. "What if he'd really hurt me? What if he'd hit a little kid?"

"So? Are you going to go to the police?" I asked.

Simon gave me a funny look. "No, Sam. The police are coming to us."

Oh yeah. I forgot.

"And on Thursday, I'm going to give them my time sheet," Simon told me. "They'll know what to do."

On Wednesday night, Simon came over to my house. We worked on our project a bit, then we got out the thousand dollars.

"I've been thinking," said Simon. "We just can't keep this money. We've got to tell somebody about it."

I closed my fist around the wad. Man! I did *not* want to hand it over to anybody.

"We can't spend it," said Simon. "Everyone would ask where we got so much money."

"I know," I said. "But I just like looking at it.

Holding it. Just dreaming about what I could buy."

Simon nodded. "But I've got an idea. What if we hand it over to the police as part of our project? We'd really surprise everyone. And we'd get a great mark! What do you think?"

Well, if I *had* to give up the money, it wasn't a bad idea. In fact, Simon was pretty smart. Then, I thought of something.

"Hey!" I yelled. "Maybe we'll get a reward!"

And so we agreed on it. I said I'd go home for lunch and bring the money back with me. We didn't want to walk around with a thousand dollars all day at school.

So, guess what? I ran home at lunchtime. I opened up my desk. No money!

What?! I dumped the drawer out on the floor. No money. I looked everywhere. I knew that I had put the money in there. Where was it? Who took it?

I ran back to school to tell Simon the bad news. He didn't believe me.

"Oh, come on, Sam. Do you think I'm going to

fall for a stunt like that? You're just keeping the money for yourself. You're being a jerk!"

"No! Really. It wasn't there. You saw me put it away. It's gone."

Simon gave me a dirty look.

And then it was time for our presentation. We began with all the boring stuff first, before the police showed up for the fun stuff.

"Okay," I said to start our presentation. "Say you're in trouble. Who are you going to call?"

"Your mommy?" yelled out Jim Brody.

All the kids laughed.

"The police, that's who," said Simon.

"Yeah, and let me tell you," I said, "our work is really tough. Like, we might get a call in the middle of the night to go on a stake-out."

Mr. Chong broke in. "Are you telling us that you work with the police, Sam?"

"Well, I have, in the past," I said. "When Simon and I caught some crooks and stuff."

"But you don't really *work* with them, right, Sam?" asked Mr. Chong.

"Well . . ." I started to say. Simon hissed at me to shut up.

Then Simon read from our report. He told the kids a few things about how you get to be a cop. He talked about how long you have to go to school. Then I said a few things about the kinds of work that cops get to do.

I could see everyone was starting to get bored. I looked at my watch. It was exactly 1:45. The cops were supposed to be here.

"And when you call 911, who's going to show up at your door?"

Then someone knocked at the classroom door. Perfect timing!

I opened the door . . . but it was only the principal.

"Sam. Simon," he said. "The police are waiting for everyone downstairs."

Downstairs? Why didn't they come up? I thought fast. Maybe the cops had shown up in their new patrol cars. Maybe they were going to take us all on a high-speed chase!

"Okay, everyone," I said. "Let's go. You are about to see how the police do their work." And we all trooped down the stairs.

I was leading the way. When I turned the corner into the schoolyard, I stopped so fast that everybody banged into everybody else. I couldn't believe what I saw.

One cruiser was out on the street.

And two police officers were sitting on two really big horses in the schoolyard!

All the kids were pushing around me to see.

"Oh wow! Oh cool!" I heard kids say.

Officer Brannon got down off her horse. "I guess you know all about the stable we have at 14 Unit," she said.

"No," said Mr. Chong. "Sam and Simon didn't mention it."

We shrugged. It must have been in the stuff we didn't get around to reading.

"Not every unit has a stable," explained Officer Brannon. "We do because of all the parks in this neighborhood. Horses allow us to patrol in the park."

Then the kids asked lots of questions. Jim had a real nosey question.

"Is it true that Sam helps you with police work?" he asked.

One policeman looked over at me. It was the cop who hauled me back to school last week.

"Sam says that he's been helping you clean up the neighbourhood," said Jim Brody.

Uh-oh.

The big cop smiled at me. "We wouldn't want to give away any police secrets," he said. "But Sam will soon be working on a really nasty case."

Huh?

"Come here, Sam. Show the kids how you help out with some street-level police work."

Huh?

I watched as the policeman walked over to the cruiser.

"Officer Singh," he said, "would you please hand Sam our street-level clean-up tool?"

I watched as Officer Singh got a broom and dustpan out of the trunk.

"Here you go, Sam," said the policeman. "Time to show these kids how you go about cleaning up the streets."

He pointed to the horses. Then he pointed to the ground beneath the horses. Then he pointed to what was on the ground beneath the horses.

"We call them 'road apples,'" explained Officer Brannon. "Better get started."

CHAPTER 8

Show-and-Tell Showdown

Simon and I swept up the mess while the other kids talked to the cops.

"You can put the . . . er . . . road apples in the hillside garden, boys," said Mr. Chong.

Simon and I finished. Then we went off behind the school.

"Why couldn't you keep your stupid mouth shut, Sam?"

"Oh, shut up yourself," I said. I was in no mood to have my best friend tell me I was stupid.

Not that he was my best friend any more.

"And I didn't keep the money. Someone took it."

"Yeah, right," Simon replied. "I've seen the way you drool all over those bills. You want it all for yourself. You don't even want to share it with me."

That's when I punched him. So then he threw the dustpan at me. So then I chased him down the hill with the broom.

"Sam! Look! The car!"

"Get down!" I hissed. The two of us dropped to our knees behind a small bush. We forgot all about fighting.

Simon pulled out his time sheet. "Go get the cops, Sam," he said. "I'll stay here and watch."

I nodded and crept away on my belly. At the top of the hill, I stood and ran back to the schoolyard. No one was there.

The horses were tied up to the bike rack. Where was everyone?

I ran back to the hill and crawled to our spot. The time sheet was there on the ground. But where was Simon?

I looked down the hill. There was Simon. The guy in the yellow car was dragging Simon into his car!

"Help!" I yelled as I ran up to the school. "Help! Help!"

No one came. No one heard me. What was I going to do?

Then I saw the horses. I don't know how to explain what happened . . . just that my best friend was in big trouble.

I climbed onto a bike seat and then jumped up on one of the horses. I'd never been on a horse before. But how hard could riding it be? I yelled, "Giddy up!"

Nothing happened.

I dug in my heels and screamed, "Yee-hah!"

The horse bucked and almost threw me off. Then it started moving. We trotted out of the yard and into the street. But I wasn't alone any more. Officer Singh jumped out of his car and yelled at me and the horse.

The horse started to gallop. All I could do was hold on.

Officer Singh got back in the cruiser and turned on the siren. He chased us down the street and around the corner. I held on to that horse with everything I had. How do you stop one of these things?

And then I saw the yellow car. I dug in my heels. "Move!" I shouted at the horse. We raced after the car and Simon.

Suddenly the yellow car braked to a stop. I was almost on top of it. I slipped and slid and fell off the horse.

Officer Singh jumped out of the cruiser and grabbed me.

"What's going on?" he yelled.

I shook myself loose. "That guy has got Simon! He kidnapped my friend!"

Just then Simon opened the car door and tumbled out onto the street.

"What happened?" I shouted. "How did he get you in the car?"

Simon got to his feet. "He was starting to drive away, so I ran down the hill. He saw me and when I got there, he kidnapped me," Simon said.

"I didn't kidnap nobody," shouted the driver. "I just wanted to talk to you, kid. I wanted to know why you and your little friend were watching me. I just wanted to tell you not to be so nosey." He turned to Officer Singh. "That's all, officer. I was just having some fun with the kid."

"Oh yeah?" said Simon. Then he reached back into the car. "Look!" Simon said. And he held up little bags of white powder.

Drugs! So that's what this was all about. The

guy had been selling drugs to the high school students. And we had Simon's snotty time sheet to prove it!

Things happened fast after that. Officer Singh read the guy his rights and snapped handcuffs on him. He threw him into the cruiser and took off.

By now, everyone else was outside. Officer Brannon took us back to the school. The principal phoned our parents. When they arrived, Officer Brannon told us to start from the beginning.

So we did. The whole story. Even about the money.

"And where's the money now?" asked my mom.

"It was in my desk drawer," I said. "But now it's gone. Someone took it. That's the truth, I swear."

"Sure, kid," said Officer Brannon.

"It *is* the truth," said Simon. "If Sam says so, it's the truth."

"Thanks, buddy," I whispered.

"Wait a minute," said my mom. "I think I might know where the money went." She turned to the principal. "Can you get Ellen out of class, please?"

Ellen? Who needs that little brat around? But when Ellen showed up, the mystery was solved.

"I saw you in Sam's bedroom this morning, Ellen," said my mom. "Did you take anything?"

Ellen nodded. Then she explained. "I needed pencil crayons. For my autumn leaves project. Sam never uses his."

"Did you take any money out of his drawer?" my mom asked.

"Yes," said Ellen. "And I put it back where it belongs."

"What are you talking about?" I yelled.

"*Duh!* In the Monopoly game, you dummy," answered Ellen.

"What?" I yelled again.

But Officer Brannon began to laugh. "You put real money into a board game?"

Ellen shook her head. "It wasn't real money. Where would Sam get *real* hundred-dollar bills?"

So my mom hugged Ellen. My dad and Officer Brannon went to our house to find the Monopoly game. They were back in a few minutes with ten one-hundred-dollar bills. One thousand dollars. It looked a little drooled over.

Not long after that, a couple of reporters showed up. Sam and me got our pictures in the newspaper and were on the TV news, just like old times. A few days later, we were given medals for stopping crime in the neighborhood. We even got a small reward. Fifty bucks each. Not enough to buy everything I'd dreamed about, but not too shabby, either.

By the way, we got an "A" on our report.

Or a "Y," if you're a Bat.

Sharon Jennings is the author of more than fifteen books for young people. Her first success was a picture book, *Jeremiah and Mrs. Ming*, illustrated by Mireille Levert. Since then, Sharon has written five other picture books, including *Priscilla and Rosy* and *Priscilla's Pas de Deux*, both illustrated by Linda Hendry.

Sharon has already created three books about the Bat Gang: *Bats and Burglars, Bats in the Garbage* and *Bats out the Window*. This book is her fourth "Bats" novel.

Sharon says, "There is nothing I like to do more than write. I become the characters and live inside their story." In real life, Sharon Jennings balances her writing life with being a mother to three teenage children. She lives in Toronto but frequently visits schools across Canada and in the United States. For more information, visit her website at www.sharonjennings.ca.